Captains and Cranberries

Captains and Cranberries

A True Tale
of
Old Cape Cod

Charles Nordhoff

edited by
Edward Lodi

ROCK VILLAGE
PUBLISHING

Middleborough, Massachusetts
First Printing

Captains and Cranberries

Copyright © 2008 by Edward Lodi

Typography and cover design by Carolyn Gilmore

ISBN-13: 978-1-934400-04-3
ISBN-10: 1-934400-04-1

Rock Village Publishing
41 Walnut Street
Middleborough MA 02346
(508) 946-4738
rockvillage@verizon.net

Acknowledgment

Captains and Cranberries originally appeared (in a slightly different form) under the title "Mehetabel Rogers's Cranberry Swamp" in a volume of short stories by Charles Nordhoff titled *Cape Cod and All Along Shore* (New York: Harper & Brothers, Publishers, 1868).

Dedication

The editor dedicates this book to those ships' captains, sailors, lighthouse keepers, and their wives and daughters of old Cape Cod who braved the elements on the seas and along the shores, and who had the fortitude and foresight to undertake new ventures.

CONTENTS

Captains and Cranberries

INTRODUCTION

TWO YOUNG MEN OF CAPE COD—brothers who are also close friends, one a captain of a fishing vessel and the other soon to be a captain—are rivals for the hand of the same young woman. This situation provides the basis for the plot of *Captains and Cranberries*, a rousing tale of adventure, hardship, disaster, and heroism at sea.

So much for the *Captains* part. But what about the *Cranberries*?

Well, anyone familiar with the history of Cape Cod knows that there has long been a close association between the captains, or skippers, of sailing vessels, and cranberries. It was enterprising ships' captains, who, on Cape Cod in the early decades of the nineteenth century, first undertook the cultivation of this very American berry.

There were a number of reasons for this. Wild cranberries grew abundantly on the Cape; so did seafaring men. If you were a male born and bred on Cape Cod in the early eighteen hundreds, chances were you earned your livelihood from the sea. The healthier, hardier, luckier, more enterprising men became captains of their own ships; the same qualities that made them successful leaders of men made them successful pioneers in this new branch of agriculture. ("Where promotion goes by merit the captain is apt to be the better man.") And sea captains, besides possessing the courage and insight necessary for new and risky ventures, were also likely to possess the wherewithal—the money—that was likewise needed.

Interestingly enough, though, it is not a captain, but a captain's *wife* who, in *Captains and Cranberries*, has the foresight to envision the profits to be made from cultivating the lowly cranberry. Mehetabel Rogers is married to a former sea captain (now a light-house keeper) too old and set in his ways to risk their hard earned savings on a cranberry "swamp." ("Everybody knew that cranberries would presently be worth no more in Boston than beach plums. And then where would all the dollars be which silly people buried in swamps!") So she turns to a young and energetic captain, just starting out in life, for the capital needed to convert two acres of worthless swampland into a wealth-producing cranberry patch.

Oh, did I mention that Mehetabel is the mother of Rachel, the young woman whom the two brothers would each like to marry? And that...well, perhaps it's best that I let the reader discover for him- or herself just what the story is all about. I will say this, though: *Captains and Cranberries* is a compelling tale, full of nautical adventures, romantic rivalries, plot twists, tragedies, hardships, and triumphs.

It is also about the early days of cranberry farming, and fully captures the flavor of old Cape Cod.

Moreover, it is a true story, or so the author claims, and there is no reason to doubt his word. Certainly the names of the characters—Rogers, Robbins, Nickerson, Baker, Snow—are familiar Cape Cod names even today.

I discovered *Captains and Cranberries* while browsing in a used bookstore on Cape Cod. It is included in a collection of seven short stories by Charles Nordhoff called *Cape Cod and All Along Shore*. Its original title was "Mehetabel Rogers's Cranberry Swamp." I've changed it to *Captains and Cranberries* to more accurately reflect its theme and content; it's more about the sea than about a cranberry patch, though the latter does play a significant role and is referred to throughout.

The book appeared in 1868. However, the story first saw publication sometime before that, in *Harper's Magazine*, or possibly in the *Atlantic Monthly*. (The author, in his preface, is not clear on the subject.)

Those readers familiar with the name Charles Nordhoff are probably thinking of the grandson, co-author of a number of nautical adventure novels, including *Mutiny on the Bounty*.

Our Charles Nordhoff (the grandfather)—whose shade I trust I have not offended by changing the name of his admirable story—was born in 1830 in Prussia, but spent a good part of his younger years as an American sailor. He wrote about his experiences in a number of compelling books: *Man-of-War Life* (1855), *The Merchant Vessel* (also 1855), *Whaling and Fishing* (1856), and *Stories of the Island World* (1857).

From 1861 to 1871 Nordhoff was editor of the New York *Evening Post*. He served as Washington correspondent for the New York *Herald* from 1874 to 1890. Many of his later books are social histories based on the knowledge and experience gained in those journalistic years.

Besides the title, I've made a few minor (I stress the word *minor*) changes, to make the story more accessible to modern readers. Most significant, I've divided it into brief chapters, and assigned my own titles to those chapters. By doing so I hope to convey something of the nautical and historical nature of the story to readers who might otherwise "pass" on a long short story or a short novel (i.e., a novella) called, simply, "Mehetabel Rogers's Cranberry Swamp." (Doesn't sound very nautical.)

I've also taken the liberty (forgive me, Charles!) of altering the spellings for a few of the dialect words of some of the more "Cape Cod" speakers. For instance, "ef" in the original becomes "if" in my version and "sich" becomes "such." I felt the author's renderings, when strung together in a sentence, were too distracting, perhaps too obfuscating, for the modern reader. A comparison to the original (if you can find it; it's a rare book) will show that I've made changes in only a handful of instances.

Lastly, I've made minor (very minor) changes in punctuation, to bring it more in line with modern usage.

Edward Lodi
Middleborough MA

THE FOLKS AT
NAUSET LIGHTS

"MAN PROPOSES, GOD DISPOSES." So says an old proverb. Sometimes women propose.

Mehetabel Rogers proposed to go to Boston tomorrow. She had been there once before in her life, for Boston is a long way off, and the Old Colony Railroad runs only to Barnstable as yet; and Mehetabel Rogers lives below Chatham, on old Cape Cod.

Captain Rogers was light-house keeper at Nauset. There are three lights there to look after; they stand on a high bluff, at the foot of which washes the Atlantic, while back of it stretches a sandy plain, the greater part of which is yet "Congress land," which our Uncle Samuel does not find easy to sell, even at a shilling an acre. Captain Rogers was a sailor, that you might see at the first glance.

He was a ship captain, not a militia captain; that is to say, he had been a ship captain, now he was a shore captain, and lights were his ship. It made little difference to him, so far as responsibility went, or work either; for though he had no longer a lee-shore to fear for himself, every easterly gale made him fidget at his lights, thinking of the poor fellows who might be warned off by their gleam; and for the rest, his observations, which were formerly taken at noon, were now made at midnight; where he would before have got a pull on the main-sheet, he now ordered a rub of the lantern glasses; and if he had no dead-reckoning to work up, he yet kept a log, no light job to an old tar whose fingers are handier at a long splice or a timber hitch than at pot-hooks and hangers.

Captain Rogers was a man of regular habits, for you see, a light-house keeper is a responsible person. He is not like a Governor of State, or a member of the Cabinet, who has all night in, and has only to sign letters, and order things done which are of no consequence when they are done. A light-house keeper must keep his lights bright, and if he should be a careless person, or a sleepy-head, or, perhaps, even a lover of strong drink, don't you see, some night a poor mariner, steering for his light in fullest confidence, would run his ship ashore, and perhaps lose his crew as well as his cargo.

From which you will quickly gather that only the most trusty men in the State ought to be appointed light-house keepers, and a man who could not be elected hog-reeve in his town ought to be ashamed of himself for asking the Secretary of the Treasury, who knows no better, poor ignorant creature! to trust him with a light.

I advise you not to ask Captain Rogers if he could be elected hog-reeve. That is beside the matter.

"I wish you weren't going to Boston," said the Captain, for the twentieth time, on the evening of the day before Aunt Mehetabel was to set out. She was packing up, and it made him nervous to see now one thing and then another, now a comb, and then a piece of molasses cake, and then a pair of stockings, slipped into the carpet-sack which was to accompany the good lady on her journey.

"Too late," she said, catching up a hymn book, which her eye happened to light upon just then, and putting it into a handy pocket in the all-containing bag, by way of light reading.

"Seems to break up everything so," groaned Uncle Rogers. "I don't see what's the use of Boston."

"You ain't going," was the triumphant reply, as a shiny and well-preserved pair of shoes were hauled out of a corner and crammed into the bag.

Aunt Mehetabel was determined not to be vexed with the old man. She was going to Boston; she was sure of that, and why should she lose her temper? *Men is such poor, helpless creatures. If they don't have everything just so, they get all upset, and no more use 'n a codhook without a bait.*

"Now then, old man, there's the oil, and there's the wick, 'nd there's your clothes for the lanterns, 'nd there's the gal, she knows how to cook as well as her marm. Now then, lets turn in, for you've got to drive me

11

over to the stage soon as you put out your lights in the morning."

The gal's name was Rachel, and she was pretty. There are a good many pretty girls on old Cape Cod. A Cape man once told me in confidence that in all his voyages he had not seen such women as they breed on the Cape, and I think he was right. Rachel was not only pretty; she could cook, as her mother said; she could iron a shirt, and wash it too; she knew how to clean the lantern glasses, all except the last finishing touch, which the old Captain administered himself, with a cloth locked up in a separate locker.

Rachel was "hanging round the room," her mother said, "as though she expected a feller."

Poor child! Her "feller" was in Boston, getting ready for a voyage to the Bank Querau after cod; and Rachel was "hanging round" in hopes that she might, at the last moment, gain permission of her mother to go along in the stage tomorrow.

Captain Aleck
of the *Lucy Ann*

ALECK NICKERSON WAS CAPTAIN OF THE *LUCY ANN*, banker; and the *Lucy Ann* was getting her outfit in Boston for an early start to the Banks. Captain Aleck was determined to fish for "high line" out of Chatham; it was his first voyage as master, and he was what they call a "fishy man"—not a man given to incredible stories, but one who meant to fill his ship, or to "wet his salt," as they say.

He had selected a good crew, and his brother was his mate. Down in Chatham, people said that the *Lucy Ann* was likely to come home with a good stint of fish.

It used to puzzle the gossips which of the two it was that Rachel Rogers favored, whether Aleck, or Mulford his brother. I am not sure that she knew herself. Aleck had committed the indiscretion of almost offering himself to her; and her mother had been rash enough to say once that Aleck Nickerson was a "likely feller;" which makes me think that Mulford had the best chance just then. But the two were always together; and some people pretended to say that they went courting in common, and that either would have been satisfied with the other's success.

Cape folk are not cold-blooded, but they are careful. There is an old rule, never to dance with the mate if you can dance with the captain, which is sound enough so far as I know. Some young women, who live by rule, follow this one among others, and I have known them to profit by its observance. In a cold country and a barren, where bread and butter are not over plentiful, the captain's house has perhaps attractions which the mate's has not; and women, as everybody knows, have to live a great deal indoors. But where promotion goes by merit the captain is apt to be the better man; and, so being, he has a right to the prettiest girl, which no pretty girl I ever knew would dispute. So that, perhaps, after all, Captain Aleck had the best chance.

How Cranberries Saved Cape Cod

A UNT MEHETABEL ARRIVED SAFELY IN BOSTON, and at once took charge of the *Lucy Ann*'s cabin. She had a plan to talk over with Captain Aleck, a plan which had occurred to her during her last visit to Harwich.

At this time the gradual failure of the fish, and the somewhat rapid increase of the population of the Cape, caused a good deal of uneasiness to the people of that thrifty region. All the young men and most of the old fellows are fishermen; the whole living of the Cape is taken from the ocean. Hitherto there had been abundance for all, according to their frugal expectations; but now the prospect grew dark. The great fish days off Chatham were no longer what they had been in former years. The fleet, which was formerly always "hauled up" before Thanksgiving Day, now cruised anxiously after the missing schools till far into December, and could not find them; and the Banks no longer furnished codfish in the wonted abundance.

And yet every Cape boy is a born sailor and fisherman. They are a web-footed race; and, to add to the difficulty, a curiously home-loving race. Any other people would have emigrated. The California and Oregon coasts yield fish in such abundance as no Cape man ever even dreamed of, and to a sailor the world is open. But to these curious Cape men there is no place in the world so beautiful or so dear as their own flat, sandy, tide-washed waste, where the corn scarcely grows breast-high, and the sand is ankle-deep in the best cultivated garden.

Once Uncle Shabael Robbins drove me out in his hay wagon, and coming to a knoll a little higher and a little greener than the surrounding flats, the enthusiastic old fellow cried out, in great exultation, "Let us stop and look around: far's you've traveled, I know you never saw so fine a piece of country as this!"

Place him where you will, in the most fertile and beautiful part of the globe if you please, and the Cape Cod man will sigh wearily for his sand, his pine needles, and the moan of the ocean on his flat beach. That is in the nature of the creature, and you can not change it.

Given, then, that no one would move away; that all were bent on fishing; that, in fact, this was the only possible employment for the mass of the people, and the single source of their prosperity; and finally that there were not fish for all the fishermen: and you will understand that the old folks began to fear a famine for the next generation, and to talk drearily of the fading glories of the Cape.

Just at this time an ingenious Yankee invented the cranberry culture, and saved the Cape. The cranberry is a fruit which grows best on swamp lands which can be overflowed at will with fresh water. It is an amphibious berry, which dwindles and becomes diseased if deprived of an occasional soaking. It is the God-send therefore to a people living in the midst of fresh-water ponds, and a third of whose land lay in worthless swamp, dear at a dollar an acre, useless to all, and owned only because it was a part of the place.

Enoch Doane read about cranberry swamps in his agricultural paper, saw that the berries were in good demand in the Boston market, made a careful calculation overnight, and next morning rode out and bought a dozen acres of the worst-looking swamp land in the neighborhood of Harwich.

It took him a year to prepare a ten-acre lot. He had to cut drains, to build proper flood-gates, to clear the land of the rank growth of scrub oak which covered it, to cart away a foot deep of the sour top earth, to carry on new soil, to cover that with a layer of white beach sand, and lastly to set out his berries. He laid out three hundred dollars on each acre of his "patch," and the neighbors united to call him a fool.

In three years he was a rich man, swamp lands were worth fifty dollars per acre, and the Cape was saved from starvation.

A PARTNERSHIP
IS FORMED

N OW AUNT MEHETABEL HAD HEARD OF ENOCH DOANE'S
folly, which was in everybody's mouth. She knew
he was a shrewd old fellow; and one day she
rode down to Harwich in the stage to inspect his opera-
tions. She came back the next day in a fluster, and before she ate her dinner had selected the site for a cranberry patch of her own.

The question was, how to raise money enough to
get a couple of acres under cultivation. The old light-
house keeper had money in the bank; but he plainly
told his wife he meant to keep it there. If Enoch Doane
was a fool he was not; everybody knew that cranberries
would presently be worth no more in Boston than beach
plums. And then where would all the dollars be which
silly people buried in swamps!

Fortunately for Aunt Mehetabel the berry fever had
not yet got so far down as Nauset, and she was able to
buy her two acres of well selected but tangled swamp for

little more than a song. Her own savings, from knitting socks, and entertaining chance strangers, were sufficient for that. But how to get it into cultivation? How to clear it of that mass of scrub oak and rank stringy grass which now made it an impregnable fortress? How to pay for drains, and flood-gates, for the much digging, and carting, and hoeing, and planting, which must precede a crop?

Captain Aleck Nickerson had a little money in the bank, and from him, as one of her nearest neighbors, and confidential friends, she resolved to get help. All winter she had done her best to infect him with her own enthusiasm; and now she had come to Boston to make a last effort with him.

"If I had just five hundred dollars I'd have the pesky swamp all cleared and set out before you come back with your first fare," she said.

"But I want to build my house, Aunt Mehetabel," replied the Captain.

"You hain't got nobody to put in it, Aleck."

"Never you mind about that," retorted the Captain with a smile. "How's Rachel?"

"Rachel's ready to wait," she said. "Besides, you haven't asked her."

"Wait till I come back, high line," Aleck said, smiling.

"By that time I can have the patch clear as the palm of your hand."

"You won't get your money back in three years."

"But the first crop'll build you two houses, Aleck."

"I don't want but one, old lady, and a pretty gal to live in it."

"You young fellers is always thinking 'bout pretty gals. I swear, if I was a man I'd think of something else."

"Cranberries, Aunt Mehetabel?" queried Captain Aleck, who was lazy and inclined to tease, and besides owed a grudge to the old woman because she had left Rachel at home.

"Yes, cranberries," she replied. "Cranberries is worth ten dollars a barrel, and an acre'll yield fifty barrels easy."

"And the worms'll eat 'em before you pick 'em," Aleck said.

"And your wife'll get cross and ugly," said Aunt Mehetabel.

"And half crazy about cranberry swamp," Aleck said, with an irrepressible chuckle, swinging himself suddenly from the transom, where he was lying, through the open skylight on deck.

"You're a fool, Aleck Nickerson!" the old woman screamed after him. "O Lordy, what fools men be! Here, you boy, you lazy hound, split some wood quick. Here's ten o'clock, and no dinner on the fire. See if I don't worry him into it!" she grumbled to herself, as she poured a mess of beans into the pot.

It is unnecessary to recount the further strife between these two; the reader already knows, if he has a proper notion of what an ambitious middle-aged woman can do if she once sets her heart upon a matter, that Aunt Mehetabel won the battle. The Captain was not averse to the speculation; he had five hundred dollars laid aside on interest; he had no doubt of the success of the enterprise.

Cranberries were a "sure thing," as he well knew.

The difficulty was here: he had determined to build himself a house that fall; the place was chosen and already bought; and he intended that while the house was building he would court Rachel Rogers, and when it was finished he would marry her and stay at home that winter, as he could easily afford to do if he had only moderate luck on the Banks.

The prospect was an alluring one; like most of the enterprising young fellows on the Cape, he had been going "south," that is to say, to the West Indies, or the Brazils, or Demerara, or Mobile, every winter, to make up the year's work; and the thought of staying at home, in a snug house of his own, all winter, with a pretty young wife, while other fellows were freezing their fingers and toes on the coast, or toiling among molasses hogsheads or cotton bales in the South, was one not lightly to be given up.

But "you must keep on the right side of your mother-in-law—at least till you marry your wife," says an old proverb; and Captain Aleck gave way, and made up his mind to go another, and perhaps another winter South, and build his house the grander when the cranberries came in. As he sailed out of the harbor Aunt

Mehetabel stood on the dock, her precious bank bills tightly clutched in her hand.

"Remember us both to Rachel, Auntie," said Aleck, pointing toward his brother on the forecastle, "and don't lose the ribbon I sent her." And so they sailed off for the Banks.

THE CRANBERRY PATCH

I WOULD NOT LIKE TO HAVE BEEN one of the poor fellows whom Aunt Mehetabel employed to work on her cranberry patch. She looked after them sharply. She did not spare her own hands from the toil, and you may be sure no one else was spared. Even the old Captain was induced to devote his spare hours to the work, which went on rapidly, though slowly enough to the old woman's eager temper.

She was determined to surprise Captain Aleck on his return; and before the end of July the whole two-acre lot was cleared and fenced, and a small part of it was already of that strange unearthly white which surprises and disgusts one who sees for the first time a Cape Cod cranberry plantation.

The drains were neatly cut, the flood-gates securely built, and before the autumn frosts she hoped to have the whole ground in readiness for planting.

"Miss Rogers is a hard boss," grumbled the two

men who cleared, and dug, and carted fresh earth on to this waste; but "Miss Rogers" was a general who led her troops, and looked very sharply after skulkers.

THE WHITE DARKNESS

MEANTIME, WHILE RACHEL COOKED, and washed, and ironed, and kept house like a well-trained Cape girl, the *Lucy Ann* was fast anchored on the Banks, and her brace of lovers were such unsightly objects, covered with fish gurry, clad in oil-skins, stamping about in huge sea-boots, and enveloped in barvil and sou'wester and awkward fish-mittens, that she would scarcely have recognized them

There are Sundays on fish-ground, when all hands shave, and wash, and clean-shirt themselves—if the weather happens to be fine, that is to say. But if it is rough, a pipe and an old novel and the warm bunk in the cabin are preferred; and the most that is done to renovate the outer man is to wash in warm water and wrap in clean rags the sore fingers which a good fish day produces.

Aleck Nickerson was commonly a lucky man; he struck fish if anybody did. He lifted his anchors less often than most men; and he had a crew that could catch fish if any were within reach of their skillfully contrived baits. But this time his usual luck seemed to forsake him. He dropped his cod-lead in vain. "Picking fishing," one fish in an hour, and small at that, was the best which fell his way.

Nothing is so disheartening as poor luck in fishing; men lose even their skill, as their confidence oozes out at their fingers' end; and it is only the most sagacious who have the wit to keep their temper, and saw their lines on the rail with the patience which is sure to win in the end.

One day Captain Aleck anchored and struck fish; but not in such abundance as he desired.

"I'll go down in the boat. Lower away there, two or three of you," he said at last. "I'll try 'em a little way off; it's clear weather."

The day was almost cloudless, as fair and smooth as a calm June day off Sandy Hook. The boat was lowered, and Captain Aleck jumped into it with a bucket full of good baits and his codcraft, and pulled away about a mile off, where he had no sooner dropped his lead than he got a bite. The men on board watched him, greedily, for half an hour, sawing their own lines the while across the rail, when, suddenly, they too "struck a school," and in a moment every man was hauling in a twenty pounder.

The Captain was forgotten in the excitement, until the cook chanced to stick his head out of the companionway, who cried out, "Why, it's as thick as mush!"

So it was. The treacherous fog had settled down

all at once, as it often does on the Banks; and where a short half hour ago all was clear as a bell, now you could not see the jib-boom end.

"Where's the Skipper?" was the question, as all hands held up a moment and stared in each other's faces.

"Ring the bell, quick, some one!" said Mulford. "Skipper's all right. He'll be along soon as he hears the sound." Nevertheless, Mulford went forward himself, and with an iron belaying-pin beat lustily on the fluke of the spare anchor.

"Hold up a minute," he said, presently. "Listen, everbody!"

The men stopped talking and bent their ears to the rail; but they heard no plashing of oars, no shout through the white darkness.

"Shout. Sing out all together, now!" Mulford ordered. They "sung out" from all throats, then listened again, eagerly, for an answering cry. But none came.

"Ring the bell there, somebody, and ring loud," Mulford said. "He'll be here, directly."

Somebody rung, and somebody beat the anchor, while another man climbed to the masthead, to see if he could peer above the fog, and perhaps beyond it; but he came down shaking his head, and declaring that it was thicker up there than down on deck.

Mulford slid down on the dolphin-striker and stretched his head along the surface of the ocean, hoping to get a glimpse in that way, but in vain.

"Sh—sh!" said Uncle David Meeker, suddenly. "I

heard a cry."

In a moment all was still, and presently there came a wail; but it was from the masthead, and was the lonely voice of a sea-bird welcoming the companionship of man in the thick fog.

"It's only a gull," someone said.

"Good God, this is dreadful! Shout again, men. Sing out loud, every man. What would mother say if she was here?" muttered Mulford.

They shouted again and again. They rung the bell and beat the anchor. They listened as men listen on whose hearing depends the life of a shipmate.

"How did the boat bear?" asked the cook.

"Nor-north-east," was the reply. "Let's up anchor and look after him. Maybe he laid to his line when the fog come up."

"Not yet," was Mulford's reply. "He might have drifted apast us, and then we'd be leaving him."

But now the wind began to sigh through the shrouds, and the little *Lucy Ann* began to roll with the swell which foretold an approaching gale. Her crew looked at each other with solemn faces. In such a fog, once miss the direction, once get out of ear-shot, and the chances are slim of ever finding your ship again.

They went to the windlass presently and hove out the anchor, set the mainsail and jib, and cruised about, making short tacks through the fog, and shouting and listening by turns.

All hands remained on deck. The cook in vain cried

out, "Sate ye, one half"—the customary call to dinner on a Cape fishing schooner. The dinner was put away untasted. The growing anxiety for their Captain kept every man at his post. The fog did not lift. It began to drive, thick and fast, as the north-east wind blew up, and presently the swash of the sea against the bows became so loud as to make any cry of a human voice inaudible.

Then night came on, and at last, after running half a dozen miles dead to leeward, the anchor was let go, a double watch set, and the remainder of the crew went below to their berths in silence.

A Brother's
Quandary

AND THUS CAPTAIN ALECK WAS LOST TO THE *LUCY ANN*.
To lose a man at sea, and that man the Captain, the leader of the small band, casts a gloom over the whole voyage. Mulford was a capable fellow, he knew the fish-ground as well as his brother; and by a curious turn of luck, when the north-easter blew itself out, the cod seemed to seek the little vessel whose master was drifting no one knew whither or how.

The men drew in their fish in silence; the wonted joke was omitted; and everybody heaved a sigh of relief when at last, in three weeks after the loss of Captain Aleck, the last barrel of salt was wet, the anchor was hove up for the last time, and all sail set to a fair wind for home.

And now came the most wretched days for Mulford. In the hurry of fishing, and the anxiety of caring for the vessel, his mind had been too fully occupied to leave space for thought about his brother. But now, with a fair wind to fill the sails, and no labor except to work up his reckoning, he began to think, for the first time, that he was to be the bearer of ill news—and such ill news.

How should he tell his mother who was living quietly and happily at home, waiting in confidence for her son's return, proudly thinking of him as smartest and best among the young men on her "shore" or neighborhood? How should he go to Rachel alone—he who had never visited her except in company with Aleck?

And yet it was pleasant to think that now he might win Rachel for himself. He hated himself for the thought—and yet he thought it. You cannot help thinking, that's the mischief of it; and in the midst of the most real sorrow this ugly ray of comfort obtruded itself till poor Mulford, half distracted, wished the girl at the deuce, whose pretty face made him indulge in a thought which was mean, as he felt, and which had no proper place in his grieving heart.

So long as Aleck lived Mulford had been content that Rachel should be his sister-in-law. It was not till now it occurred to him that she could be his own wife. Why not? And yet, why? Should he take advantage by his brother's death? Could he ever forgive himself the joy of such a wedding?

Mulford was not the first generous-hearted man tormented by such thoughts of unwelcome compensations for a great sorrow. And yet how unreasonable, said a voice in his heart. What is done is done. Aleck was lost. Should he, for a punctilio, cast away what he felt would be a happiness for him? Should he leave to some stranger that which Aleck would have most certainly preferred him to have, under the circumstances? Was he not his brother's heir? He would inherit his savings— why not also the wife of his heart?

FAITH IN CRANBERRIES

WHEN MEHETABEL ROGERS HEARD THE NEWS she was "thrown all in a fluster," according to her own account.

"What'll Miss Nickerson do?" she cried. "What'll Rachel say, poor gal? O Lordy, what'll become of the cranberry patch?"

This last question was the most important.

She had given a summer to that barren swamp, and now it was a fair, smooth, chalky, ugly, but very promising plain, with ditches run through it, and water ready to cover it. She had spent the enormous sum of four hundred and fifty dollars upon it; and she was scared at the outlay, for whose return she and her partner would have so long to wait. She had thought with dread of the account she would have to give Aleck, and now she must render this account to Mulford—or perhaps, worse yet, to strangers, executors, lawyers! Men who were sure to understand nothing except that a frightful sum of money had been wasted, and no sign of profit appeared.

"Maybe Aleck was picked up!" she at last exclaimed,

ran for her bonnet, and set off for the Widow Nickerson's to communicate her hopeful doubt.

The two old women hugged the sweet thought to their hearts, and watched daily for some news of the lost Captain. But no news came; the first-fare men were all in and out again, and no tidings were heard; in Cape Ann no one had seen or heard of a missing boat. The second-fare men got home and fitted out for a fall cruise after mackerel.

At last it was time to give up Aleck for lost; no hope remained; and when the last banker was hauled up for the winter, Mrs. Nickerson put on black and gave up her boy for lost.

Rachel Rogers, too, was clad in mourning, but underneath the black stuff gown there beat a very contented little heart. So long as the two brothers came courting together she had had no heart in the courtship. While Aleck was near she would have surrendered to him, because he was the older of the two, and came with an air which was that of a man used to have his own way, and to be helped first. Besides he was nearest to that nest-building which, in Cape Cod life, as among the birds, precedes the wedding.

But as Mulford and Rachel sat together, talking of the brother lost, she began to find her heart warming to the brother living; and their common sorrow opened the way to a common confidence of love.

When Aleck was given up Rachel was promised to Mulford; and, to Aunt Mehetabel's satisfaction, the young fellow proved to have great faith in cranberries. He insisted that the plants should be set out that fall yet; and before the pond froze over the patch had been flooded. The work was done; and during the winter she rested and was thankful. Not only thankful, indeed, but triumphant.

She dragged the old Captain to see her work. She boasted in his ears of the bushels of crimson berries which should reward her labors and justify the outlay. She had scarcely patience to wait till spring.

How's All at Home?

THE SPRING CAME. Mulford was off to the Banks in a new vessel. The swamp was drained, and the cranberries were in bloom, when, one day, Captain Aleck Nickerson walked into his mother's house, sat down on a chair in the kitchen, and said, "How's all at home?"

The poor mother thought at first she saw a ghost, but when she felt her boy's arms around her she fell away in a happy swoon.

While Aleck was yet busy with her there came into these two—Rachel Rogers. She gave a little scream of terror when she saw her old lover, and, obeying the first impulse, ran out of the house. But presently she turned and came back. She could not leave Captain Aleck alone with his fainting mother; he needed help. And for the rest—she must see him at some time. But as she walked slowly back to the door, how her heart hardened toward the poor fellow within!

What business had he to come back? she was saying to herself.

"Glad to see you've come back safe, Captain Nickerson," she said to Aleck as she stepped into the kitchen again.

"All right, Rachel," said he, looking up. "But first let's get the old woman to rights. I hope my dropping in on her hain't killed her."

The poor old mother presently came to herself. She clung to her son, whom the deep had given up; but as she gathered her thoughts in order, and saw Rachel standing there, with stony face, her joy was distracted by the thought of the changes which a year had produced.

"We thought you were dead, boy," she said, fondly smoothing his hair.

"You see I'm as live as any man of my size and weight," replied Aleck, shaking himself to prove that he was real flesh and blood.

"Go home, Rachel, and tell your mother," said she, dismissing the young girl, who turned and went out silently.

"What's the matter with Rachel?" asked Captain Aleck. "She don't seem glad to see me back."

"She thought you was lost, my son."

"And then?"

"She's promised to Mulford, my son," the old woman said, looking at him anxiously. "But oh, Aleck, I'm so happy! Don't mind her. Look at me. It was so weary without you, boy."

Captain Aleck sat himself down silently in a chair

beside her. It was not such a coming home as he had looked forward to.

"Where's Mulford, mother?" he asked, after awhile.

"He's got a new vessel, and he's gone to the Banks."

"Did he do well last year?"

"Yes, he was lucky. He made money. But he grieved for you, Aleck; it was a blow to him."

"And Rachel's promised to him?"

"Yes, boy. But what makes you sit there so solemn? Why don't you look at me? Don't you see I'm glad you've come home?"

Her old eyes filled with tears of longing love. Hard-featured she was, hard-handed, wrinkled, faded, with a harsh, cracked voice—now curiously soft and womanly. She looked at him as though she feared he would fly out of the window; she studied the shadows flitting across his dark face as though her life depended upon his humor.

"Come, sit you down close by me," she said, as he began to walk about the room, and examine the walls and windows, and the dishes in the pantry. "I can't bear you out of my sight, Aleck. What's the use of bothering about that gal? I'm your mother, that bore you, and nursed you, and carried you around in my arms. I love you, Aleck; I'm glad you've come home. I've got more right to you than any gal on the Cape.

"Tell me how it was," she said presently, curious to hear how he was saved from the death which must have been so near him, and ready, too, to divert his mind from poor Rachel.

The story was simple enough. He had been able to keep his little shallop afloat till, late at night, he saw suddenly the huge hull of a ship looming through the fog, and bearing straight down upon him.

Unable to get out of her path, death seemed certain. But with a seaman's presence of mind he saw his opportunity; with a seaman's eye he measured the distance for a leap for life; and as the vast hull swept down upon his cockle-shell he jumped for the dolphin-striker, caught it, and was saved. Twice he dipped in the ocean as the ship pitched her bows under the sea-way. But at last he clambered to the bowsprit, and in on deck, where he had hard work to persuade the superstitious French crew not to throw him overboard, so scared and amazed were they at his appearance.

The ship was a French Indiaman, carrying a cargo of fish to Pondicherry. The captain set him off upon a homeward-bound American ship in the Indian Ocean. And here he was, with nearly a twelvemonth lost out of his life, as he said.

"But you're saved to your old mother," said she.

"And Rachel Rogers is promised to Mulford?" Captain Aleck said.

"You mustn't think hard on her, Aleck; gals don't know much—and she thought you was gone."

"Was it so long to wait?" he asked, conscious that he would have waited twice a twelvemonth for her.

"Mehetabel was willing, and Rachel didn't know which she liked best of you two, Aleck. You always went courting in couples."

"It's not too late to go to the Banks yet," he said, thinking aloud. "I can go down to Provincetown tomorrow, and get a pinky for myself."

"Not so soon, Aleck; not so soon, boy. I want you a little while. I want to look at you, to see how you've growed."

To the Region of
Fogs and Fish

"LORD A-MASSY! and so you've come back, Aleck
Nickerson!" shouted Aunt Mehetabel, coming into
the kitchen. "Glad to see you alive! The cranberries is all
in. Won't you come over and look at the swamp?"

"I'm going to Provincetown tomorrow to look up a
vessel fit to go to the Banks," Captain Aleck said. "I dare
say the cranberries'll keep."

"But I can't; I've got my work to show you, and the
swamp belongs to you till you get your money back,
Aleck."

"Never mind, Aunt Mehetabel. I don't want to build
my house now."

"For why don't you? Don't look grouty the first time
I see you; I'll be sorry about the money I owe you."

Poor Aleck was sadly badgered with these women.
He had expected to come home and find Miss Rachel
receive him as a lover lost and found; he heard only about
cranberry swamps. He had never thought about her

except as his own, and yet he vexed himself with the thought that his own ill luck, and not Rachel, was in fault; and that his ill humor was neither manly nor fair to her who caused it, or to his poor old mother, who was sad on his account when she ought to have been entirely happy.

"I'll send my old man over for you by and by, Aleck," Aunt Mehetabel said, feeling—the crafty old woman—that she was not likely just yet to get a good word from him.

"I'm a mean fool to be putting on a sour face, mother, about this gal," Aleck said, looking up after she was gone. "It'll be all right when I see Mulford once. Better let me go off tomorrow. This'll all wear off when I get on fish ground again."

He rode over to Provincetown in the stage next morning; found a little pink-sterned schooner laid up, which no one had thought worthy of another trip to the Banks; hauled her up, cleaned her bottom, painted it in two tides, picked up a crew, got his outfit, and in a week was on the way to the region of fogs and fish.

Before he sailed he visited the lights, and to Aunt Mehetabel's great delight expressed his satisfaction at the condition of the cranberry patch. Also he met Miss Rachel, who held out her hand to him, like a girl who bears no grudge against a discarded lover—a piece of generosity which not many young women are capable of.

"I'm going to look up Mulford, Rachel; take care of yourself till I bring him home," he said.

His heart was light once more; a week of hard work, and a foretaste of the Banks, had set his thoughts in order.

"I felt mean to you at first, Rachel," he said, as they walked out together toward the road. "But it warn't your fault, gal. And Mulford's a good fellow as ever lived."

So he sailed away.

TOSSED LIKE A HELPLESS CHIP

ONE DAY HIS LITTLE VESSEL LAY PITCHING LIKE A MAD BULL, in a north-easterly gale, with all her cable out and a rag of storm-sail fluttering in the gale, while in the high stern sat Skipper Aleck, with two or three weather-beaten fishermen in sou'westers and oiled-clothes, watching the weather. The sea was too heavy to fish, and the fog was so thick that a good lookout was necessary.

"When it broke away awhile ago I saw a vessel off yonder, to windward," David Meeker said. "It looked like Mulford's schooner, too. Had just such a kink in her topmast. But I couldn't see her but for a minute. Maybe it warn't."

"Anchored?" asked the Skipper.

"No, under way. Dreadful work to be under way such weather."

"Too thick to bang about much," Sylvie Baker said. "I'd ruther lay to anchor than under sail."

"We'll have to look out for that fellow, boys," Aleck said cheerfully. "Hope he'll not foul our hawse."

"Guess he stood across, on the starboard tack; he's all clear before this."

"Whew! How it howls!" Sylvie Baker said, as a squall burst fiercely over the little vessel, and for a moment bore her down, and held her and the sea almost still.

Just then the fog bank lifted a little, and the alert eyes of the little group peered curiously around, as the vessel rose on a great sea, in search of possible companions.

"By gracious! how wild it looks—hello! What's that?" shouted one, pointing directly to windward, where now only a great black mass of water was to be seen as the schooner sank with a receding billow.

"That's a wreck, if my old eyes is worth anything."

All hands watched eagerly. It was quite a minute before the vessel was thrown up on a sufficiently high sea to enable them to get a fair view. Then all cried, with one voice, "A wreck! a wreck!"

"Turn out there, boys!" cried Skipper Aleck down the companion-hatch. "This fellow'll be down on top of us if he don't mind!"

The sleepers tumbled out of their warm berths, and crawled into their oiled jackets and fish-boots as hurriedly as they could. It was unwelcome news which the Skipper had cried down the hatch, and some who were dressing themselves in the cabin were pale with the thought of it.

Leave them alone, and they were safe, there in the midst of the ocean, with a fierce northeaster blowing great guns, and the sea rolling mountains high—safe as though they had been sleeping with their wives at home. Let the wind howl; let the sea bellow, and hiss, and tumble their little cockle-shell about, as though it was bent on dashing her on the sand a hundred fathoms down below, and again tossing her up to the pale full moon, of which they got a glimpse overhead once in a while.

Their cable was new and strong; their little sharp-sterned craft was of a build to outride many a line-of-battle ship; only leave them alone, and these accustomed seamen ate their cold cut of beef and slept in their narrow berths as securely as any Wall Street banker in his Fifth Avenue mansion. But once slip the cable; once derange, in the middle of such a gale, the conditions on which their comfort and safety depended, and they knew that they would have such a struggle with the storm as not one but dreaded—such a battle for life as none of them could be sure of winning in.

The vessel which was drifting down upon them was about two miles away when she was first seen. She was dismasted; her mainmast was a mere stump; her foremast was swept away flush with the deck. She was tossed about like a helpless chip, a bit of rag fluttering from the stump of the mainmast barely sufficing to keep her head to the wind.

Captain Aleck and his crew watched her with eager and careful eyes. It was only at intervals they got a momentary glimpse of her. The sea ran so high that it was only when both vessels happened to be at the same time tossed upward, and when no intermediate mountain roller obstructed the sight, that they could see the helpless, dismasted craft.

"She's not anchored, Skipper," shouted David Meeker into Aleck's ear.

"No, she's drifting down on us," Aleck replied, looking nervously forward, where a few flakes of his stout hempen cable still lay flaked neatly on the deck—too few to be of use in getting out of the way of the approaching vessel.

"We can't stick out any more; there ain't enough," David shouted, in answer to his Captain's glance.

"She's going to leeward like mad; look's though she'd fetch against us, sure."

The discipline of a fishing vessel is not very strict. The men obey the captain, but they know as much as he does, and they do not always wait for orders. Every man aboard understood the necessities of the case perfectly, and it did not need Skipper Aleck's orders to set them to reefing the mainsail and foresail.

"Balance reef's the best, Skipper?" roared someone, making himself understood as well by signs.

Aleck nodded; and the sails were so reefed that only a small triangular piece of each would be exposed if it became necessary to raise them.

"Lash down the throat solid," the Skipper shouted. "Don't let anything get adrift—look out!" as a great sea swept under the schooner, and flung her for a moment nearly straight on end.

The cook's tin pans rattled drearily in the galley— a sound which those who have heard it in a great storm at sea never forget. It strikes the ears of seamen as a sign of the utmost violence of a gale.

The men at the sails were swung off their feet, and clung to the rigging with their hands till she settled down again. Those in the high stern used the moment when they were tossed to watch the fast-approaching wreck.

"She comes down on us awful fast," said Uncle David.

She was not more than half a mile away now. She had drifted a full mile in seven or eight minutes; the sea and wind were sweeping her along at the rate of not less than eight knots. In less than five minutes more it would be decided whether Captain Aleck's little *Swallow* was safe or no.

"Go forward now with your axe, Uncle David; don't cut till I tell you, old man; and stand clear when you cut. Sylvie Baker, stand by the foresail and keep your eye on me. Tell the boys to lash themselves fast. Drive half a dozen nails into this companion slide here. If we ship a sea it may wash it off else, and fill the cabin."

A Cry of
Mortal Terror

"She's not a dozen ship's lengths off now, Skipper," Job Scudder said, pointing with his finger at the schooner, on whose deck a few helpless mites could by this time be seen clinging to the bulwarks and motioning, as though dumbly entreating them for help.

There was no longer any fog to obscure the vision. The blinding spoon-drift swept constantly across, impelled with such violence by the fury of the gale that it struck the face like needle points or like sharp hail. The sea was white with foam, and the tops of the huge black mountain billows curled over in foam rifts, which broke with a hoarse, sullen roar, and were swept by or under the *Swallow* with a dull hiss, as of ten thousand venomous serpents eager for the lives of the crew.

At such times the waves no longer appear seagreen; their vast masses, rolled up by the steady fury of the wind, are dark and gloomy, as though laden with a thousand deaths; they have a restless weight and momentum; they move with the same majestic grandeur which distinguishes and makes awful the great tide which rolls over the Canadian fall at Niagara. They break slowly, and the curling top of such a wave is instantly seized by the wind and dashed, in sheets of fiercely driven drops, along the surface: this is called "spoon-drift."

As the dismasted hull swept down toward them, the crew of the little *Swallow* forgot for a moment their own peril, in watching eagerly the helpless creatures who were now so near that their faces could be seen. The wreck was almost directly ahead.

"She'll drift athwart our cable, sure, and then we're gone," old David was saying to himself, while all held their breath in dread suspense.

Just then, when their own fate seemed already sealed, a huge wave seized the hulk and carried her in one great bold sweep down past the *Swallow*'s bow. As both vessels rose on the high crest of a sea they lay for a moment abreast, and not twenty yards apart, and the two crews scanned eagerly each other's faces.

"Good God! it's your brother Mulford, Skipper!" roared the cook, who stood at Captain Aleck's side, clinging to the same shroud, and pointing to a figure, with flying hair and sea-washed clothes, which was lashed to the quarter of the wreck.

Captain Aleck had seen him already; he stood, pale and silent, looking with scared eyes at the vision, which lasted but a moment. In the next the vessel was hidden by an intervening wave; but as she disappeared a cry of mortal terror came from her crew—a cry so sharp, so full of horror that it pierced through the roaring gale, and reached even to the ear's of the *Swallow*'s men.

Well might they cry out, the hapless crew; for, with death clutching at them in every wave, they saw suddenly before their eyes the apparition of one whom the seas had swallowed up a year ago, as they believed. They saw Captain Aleck Nickerson standing there, one risen from the dead, to call them to a fate like his own.

"They've gone down!" screamed David, who had worked his way aft again; he understood the cry they had heard as the last utterance of the drowning wretches.

"Not yet—there they drift," shouted Aleck, who had leaped up on the top of the main gaff, and held himself there by the throat halyards. "There they drift, poor fellows! We can't help them now; they're too far off."

He comprehended well enough the meaning of the cry which had come from Mulford and his crew. He waved wildly with his arms toward the fast-disappearing hulk, eager to assure the poor fellows that he was no spirit summoning them to death; but his motions, if they saw them, were not calculated to reassure.

In Search of
the Wreck

THE GALE BLEW ITSELF OUT THAT NIGHT; and a sharp rain, which set in for some hours toward morning, cut down the sea so much that when the sun rose, bright and cheery, and the blue sky was once more seen, all hands were quickly called to weigh anchor and set sail in search of the wreck.

Aleck buckled on his spyglass and mounted to the main cross-trees, to look out. The wind blew lightly from the southward, and as they sailed slowly along half the crew gathered in the cross-trees and rigging, every eye scanning the horizon for some sign of the wreck.

For many hours they saw nothing; but about two o'clock in the afternoon Captain Aleck, who had tasted no food yet that day, nor felt the need of any, in his anxiety for his brother, sung out sharply, "Look out on the starboard bow there; I think I see a spar or something floating."

"Keep her away a point," he ordered the helmsman

presently, when he had viewed the object through his glass.

As they bore down upon it, it proved to be a mast, but no live thing was attached to it.

"That belongs to someone else than Mulford. It wasn't lost in this gale; see the barnacles on it," said one of the men before they came up to it.

"Haul her up again!" ordered Captain Aleck.

But presently they came to other signs of ship-wreck—floating barrels, a bucket, part of a stove boat; and at last, in the far distance, sharp-eyed David declared he saw a spar, with something like a flag waving.

"It's only the sea breaking over it," the Skipper said, nervously, not daring to give his hopes an airing in words. Yet he watched intently the piece of wreck toward which the *Swallow* was now sailing.

Certainly there was something like a fluttering rag visible on it as it was lifted by the swell; and what was that black thing which clung to the spar?

"I do believe there's a man on that wreck!" Captain Aleck shouted, suddenly, in some excitement. "Here, David, take a careful look with the glass."

"He's waving to us," David said, after some minutes. "It's a man. I see his arms waving. Now I see him trying to stand up. He sees us plainly. He is on three spars lashed together. He keeps waving, poor creature!" This much David reported in a monotonous voice, without removing his eye from the glass.

"Bring up the colors, some of you," Aleck ordered. "We'll let him know we see him, anyhow. Look sharp, there! It's not comfortable waiting on that spar for a sign from us. Get the boat ready, down there!"

"Boat's all ready, Sir," was the reply.

"O dear, how slow we do go ahead!" fidgeted the Captain at the mast-head. "Seems to me we don't get any nearer at all. There, thank God! he sees the colors. Look, David, he's sat down. Thank the Lord! he's comfortable now, poor fellow!"

"There's more wreck on the lee bow, Skipper!" sung out a man who was perched on the foremast-head. "By Godfrey, there's two men on that piece! I see 'em both. Seems to me one's dead; he don't move."

"Take hold there and launch that boat; I can't wait any longer," Aleck cried, swinging himself from the cross-trees, and sliding rapidly down on deck. "Get in here with me, Tom; it's only a quarter of a mile, and we can pull it easily."

"Keep an eye on the others, aloft there," he ordered, as they struck out from the *Swallow*. "First come first served: they'll have to wait."

The two oarsmen had no easy task before them. The sea was still high. The rain of last night had smoothed the tops of the billows; the waves no longer broke angrily, but there remained the long ground-swell, which takes always some days to subside.

The little shell of a boat was not a very safe conveyance; but Skipper Aleck did not think of safety for himself. He and his companion tugged at their oars, now forcing the boat up the great mountain-side of a long

63

wave, and presently propelled with a fearful rush into a deep pit of waters. The wind had nearly died out, and, slowly as they made headway, they progressed more rapidly than the *Swallow*, whose sails were half the time becalmed under the lee of the great seas.

"I'd give all I'll ever be worth if that was Mulford Nickerson," Captain Aleck said, half to himself. "Pull, Tom Connor; do your best. I want to see the man's face."

It was a long pull; but at last they heard a faint shout, and, turning their heads the next time the boat rose on a swell, they saw the poor fellow whom they came to save.

"All right, my man!" Aleck shouted in reply. "Look at his face, Tom Connor, and see if you know him. I can't bear to look."

"It's not your brother, Skipper," reported Tom, in a few minutes. "It's Dan'el Twyer, of Barnstable."

The poor Skipper gave a groan, but pulled ahead. "We'll make his wife glad, anyhow, please God," said he. "Hold fast, Uncle Dan'el!" he shouted. "We'll get you safe aboard directly."

With skillful management they got the boat alongside the floating spar for a moment, without knocking a hole in her bottom; and in that moment, Daniel Twyer, summoning for the effort all the little strength he had left, leaped into the stern sheets, and sank down in a heap, with dazed eyes and a frightened look, asking, "Be you alive, Aleck Nickerson, or be you a spirit?"

"He's more alive than you, you old fool!" Tom

Connor answered, gruffly, ready to quarrel with the poor fellow, now that he had saved his life. "Where's your Skipper?"

But Daniel Twyer was too weak to reply. The feeling that he was safe, that presently he would be on a ship's deck, overcame him, and he dropped insensible in the stern sheets, and was not aroused till Connor had put a bow-line under his arms, and he felt himself swung on board, and lying upon the deck of the *Swallow*.

"Keep her away for the other men!" the Captain shouted, as he leaped on board, and the boat was hauled in over the low rail of the schooner. "Now then, Dan'el Twyer, where's your Skipper?" he demanded.

"Mulford Nickerson and Zebah Snow was lashed to the main hatchway when I saw 'em last."

The wind had freshened, and the *Swallow* was running down toward the two men rapidly. David Meeker sat in the cross-trees, with the glass, watching them, and waving his hat every few minutes, to reassure their hopes.

Presently he sung out, "'Pears to me one of 'em's Zebah Snow—"

"Hurrah, boys!" Aleck shouted, his anxious face at last lighted up with joy.

"T'other one's dead," David added.

"'Tain't so!" instantly shouted the Skipper in return. "'Tain't so; if he was dead his weight wouldn't cumber the raft." And in a moment he had "shinned" to the cross-trees and held the glass to his own eye.

"'Tain't so, Uncle David," he repeated. "You don't know nothing 'bout it, old man. The other one's Mulford Nickerson, and he ain't dead, by Godfrey, for—there! I saw him move!" he shouted, at the top of his voice. "Get that boat ready to launch, down there on the deck!"

Down he slid, and in a minute was once more afloat in the boat, pulling with eager strokes for the raft, which the *Swallow* dared not approach too nearly for fear of being flung on top of it by the sea.

"Who's that on the hatch with you, Snow?" he called out, as the boat neared the raft.

The man who had been declared dead tottered half to his feet, but fell again, crying out, "Is it you, Aleck Nickerson?"

It was all he could say. The next minute Zebah Snow was jerked off the raft, and flung into the boat, and Captain Aleck stood in his place.

"Thank God, it's you, sure," said he, grasping Mulford's hands in both his; "but what's the matter?"

"My leg's broke in two places. And you're alive, dear old fellow! Thank God for that, anyhow. I don't care now. We thought it was your ghost when we drifted past you in the gale."

A BROKEN VOYAGE

THEY GOT HIM ON TO THE BOAT AND INTO THE *SWALLOW'S* cabin as carefully as they could; and here his leg was dressed, and he was cared for as tenderly as rough but kind-hearted seamen knew how.

They are a rude set, no doubt, the men of the sea, and have but little pity for the minor ails. They are merciless toward men with headaches, or nerves, or dyspepsia. They cannot believe a man sick if he can walk or eat. But there is no tenderer nurse, no more thoughtful, skillful, long-suffering, self-denying attendant on a real and serious sick-bed than the roughest old tar in the forecastle.

When Skipper Aleck had seen Mulford comfortably tucked away in his own berth, and had administered a cup of tea and such other nourishment to him as was fit and at hand, he went on deck and called his crew around him. Cod fishermen are not paid wages; each man keeps account of his own fish, and receives their value when they are sold, less a certain share reserved for the owners of the vessel, and another smaller share which the Captain has for his conduct of the voyage.

Aleck was determined to steer at once for home; but the *Swallow* was not more than half full of fish, and to make what is called a broken voyage would be a serious loss to men who had families to feed and clothe.

The seniors of the crew had already agreed upon their course, however; and when their Captain said, "Men, I want to take the *Swallow* home as fast as she can sail," David Meeker put the helm up, Tom Connor bent on the stay-sail, and with a ready, "All right, Skipper!" the little craft was put upon her proper course with all sail set.

On the tenth day they ran into Provincetown. It was a bright June day, and Mulford, who had been gradually sinking, lay upon the deck with his brother by him.

"Don't think hardly of poor Rachel," he said, for the hundredth time. "It was I that persuaded her; and God knows I was sorry for you, brother; but we all thought you dead."

"I'll dance at your wedding, dear old fellow, this winter," Aleck said.

"You'll bury me in the old graveyard next to father," replied Mulford, solemnly. "And Aleck, promise me that you'll take Rachel. She loves you now. She's a good gal. Don't let me go, feeling that I parted you two."

Aleck held the poor fellow's hot hands in his own. He did not suspect how near his brother was to death. There was not much pain in the broken leg now; but that was because mortification had set in. The fractured limb had been too badly wounded when it was jammed between two heavy floating spars, to afford hopes of recovery, even had Mulford had more skillful treatment than the poor fishermen could give him.

He died shortly after they had cast anchor; and poor Aleck, broken with grief, set out for home to carry the sad tidings to his mother.

Not a Worm Amongst 'Em

IT IS A TRUE STORY WHICH I HAVE TOLD YOU; and the poor mother who sorrowed for two sons lost at sea, and yet thanked God for one of them saved, still lives with that one who now brought home his dead brother.

The women of the Cape have need of stout hearts, for they do not know what moment their dearest are suffering the agony of death. They cannot tell what minute shall make any one of them a widow or childless. I could show you a row of white houses in a little Cape Cod village, in seven of which live the widows made by one great gale.

It is not often the greedy sea gives up its dead; it is not always, alas! that of two sons one is saved; and when the Widow Nickerson had heard all this sad tale it was not without proper cause she said, through her tears, "I've saved one, anyhow. Thank God, who took away, but who also gave me back you, my boy!"

She lives yet, this old woman, and is happy too;

for is she not spoiling a white-haired grandson, who, at three years old, is impatient to be six, that he may be cook of his father's schooner?

Rachel and Aleck sorrowed together over Mulford's death. They are now man and wife. Captain Aleck had to "go away South" for a couple of winters to restore his broken fortunes; but with this and two good fish years he gained back more than he had lost. And one Thanksgiving afternoon he went over and asked Rachel if she would marry him.

The cranberry patch in these years had borne so abundantly that Aunt Mehetabel was regarded in her neighborhood as a woman of great capacity and good luck; and when Captain Aleck came to ask her and the old light-house keeper for their daughter, she said, "Rachel's been waiting for you, Aleck; she wouldn't have none else but you—and this year's crop of berries'll build you a house."

"The worms'll eat 'em before you pick 'em," said Aleck, remembering the old bout in the *Lucy Ann*'s cabin.

"They're all picked, and not a worm amongst 'em," she replied. "And if it warn't for them cranberries you'd have to go away this winter, little as you thought it, instead of sitting comfortable in your own house. Tell you what, boy, cranberry swamp's better than going to the Banks."

If the respectable reader will accept that last sentence as a moral to this true tale he is welcome to it.